Angus
and the Cat

TOLD AND PICTURED BY
MARJORIE FLACK

SQUARE
FISH

Farrar Straus Giroux
New York

ANGUS AND THE CAT. Copyright © 1931 by Marjorie Flack Larsson, copyright renewed 1959 by Hilma Larsson Barnum. All rights reserved. Printed in China by South China Printing Company Ltd., Dongguan City, Guangdong Province. For information, address Square Fish, 175 Fifth Avenue, New York, NY 10010. Square Fish and the Square Fish logo are trademarks of Macmillan and are used by Farrar Straus Giroux under license from Macmillan. Library of Congress catalog card number: 96-61684. Originally published by Doubleday, Doran & Company, Inc., 1931. First Square Fish Edition: March 2012. Square Fish logo designed by Filomena Tuosto. mackids.com
ISBN 978-0-374-40382-9   20 19 18 17   AR: 2.7

Each day as Angus grew older he grew longer but not much higher. Scottie dogs grow that way.

Now as Angus grew older and longer he learned MANY THINGS. He learned it is best to stay in one's own yard   and

FROGS can jump   but

NOT to jump after them   and

BALLOONS go

POP!

Angus also learned NOT to lie on the sofa and NOT to take SOMEBODY ELSE'S food and things like that.

But there was SOMETHING outdoors Angus was very
curious about but had NEVER learned about, and that was

CATS.

The leash was TOO short.

Until one day WHAT should Angus
find INDOORS lying on the SOFA but
a strange little CAT!

Angus came closer—

The CAT sat up.

Angus

came

closer—

Up jumped the **CAT** onto the arm
of the sofa. Angus came closer and—

SISS-S-S-S-S-S!!!
That little CAT boxed
Angus's ears!

Woo-oo-oof—Woo-oo-oof!
said Angus.
Up jumped the CAT onto
the sofa back, up to the mantel
—and Angus was not
high enough
to reach
her!

But at lunch time down she came
to try and take Angus's food—

though not for long.

Up she jumped
onto the table,
and Angus was not
high enough
to reach
her!

At nap time there she was sitting in Angus's
own special square of sunshine—

WASHING HER FACE,

though not for long.

Up she jumped onto
the window sill,
   and Angus was not
      high enough
         to reach
           her!

For THREE whole days Angus was very busy chasing THAT CAT, but she always went up out of reach until on the fourth day he chased her UP-THE-STAIRS

into the BEDROOM and she was
completely GONE!

Angus looked under the bed —
no CAT was there.

Angus looked out of the window

into his yard,

into the next yard—no CAT could he see ANYWHERE.

Angus went DOWN-THE-STAIRS.

He looked on the sofa—no CAT was there.

He looked on the mantel—no CAT was there.

Angus looked on the table and

on the window sills—

no CAT was indoors
ANYWHERE.

So Angus was ALL-ALONE. There was no CAT to box his ears. There was no CAT to take his food. There was no CAT to sit in his sunshine. There was no CAT to chase away. So Angus was ALL-ALONE and he had NOTHING-TO-DO!

Angus missed the little CAT.

But — at lunch time he heard this noise:

PURRRRR—

and there she was again.

And Angus knew

and the CAT knew

that Angus knew

that —

Angus was GLAD the cat came back!